# NICOLA O'BYRNE

# WHAT'S NEXT DOOR?

nosy crow

# Hey!

## Where are we?

I can't see a thing in here.

Can anybody hear me?

If you're out there,

**clap** your hands

to **turn on** the light!

Thank you. That's **much** better.
But who's this?

Hey! There'll be no **eating** in **this** book!
Let's help Carter get home,
but how can we do that?

I know!
Let's **draw** a door!
Crocodiles like water,
so use your finger to **trace**
the dotted line and
**think** very hard about
somewhere **wet**.

Well done!
That's a **brilliant** door!

And Carter's off!
But – oh dear – it looks
as if it's a bit of a squeeze.

Can you **jiggle** and **wiggle** the book
to help him through?

Let's see what's next door . . .

Oh no! This **can't** be the right place.

Crocodiles like water,
but this sea is **far** too **stormy**.
Poor Carter!

Quick!
Use your finger
again and **draw** a circle.
We need a drain before
Carter ends up as fish food!

Well, that's better, but Carter's soaked through. Can you **blow** on him to dry him out? That might cheer him up a bit.

Let's try again. We need somewhere less stormy.

Draw a door with
your finger and,
whatever you do,
don't think
of the ocean!

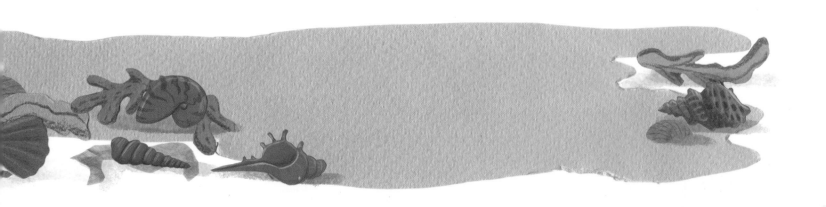

That's a **very good** door,
but crocodiles have rather **big bottoms.**

Can you **tip** the book to help him through?

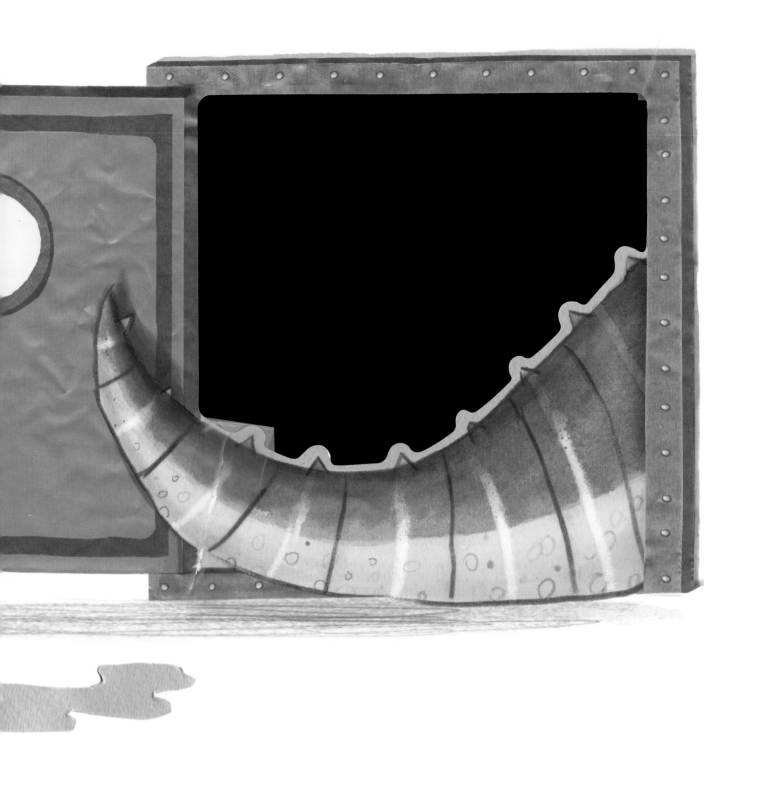

Let's see what's next door . . .

Uh-oh! This isn't the right place
for Carter either – it's **far** too **cold.**

Look at poor Carter. He's shivering!
Were you thinking of somewhere **cold?**
**Are you sure?**

I know, let's try and get rid of the snow.
Can you **turn** the book upside down
and **shake** the snow out?

**Whoops!** You made a blizzard instead.
And Carter looks really **cross.**
I do hope he isn't going to eat us.
Let's **rub** his tummy to warm him up.
That might help.

OK, let's get it right this time.

Think of
somewhere **hot**.
Super **hot**.
Extra **hot**.
Ready?
Use your finger
to **draw**
the door.

Well done **again!**
Just look at that **door!**

Do you think Carter
will fit through it?
Can you give him
a big **push?**

Let's see what's next **door . . .**

Ooh, it's **lovely** and **warm** here.
Just **perfect.**

But . . . what's wrong now?
Do you think it's **too**
**hot** for Carter?

Yep, it's definitely too **hot!**
Look, Carter's had to have a little lie down.

Quick! **Fan** him with your hand!

So, we need a place that's not **dark**,
not too **stormy**, not too **cold**
and not too **hot.**

We need to **draw**
another door!

Use your finger to trace the line and **think** very hard about somewhere that's **just right.**

# Great!

## Off we go again!

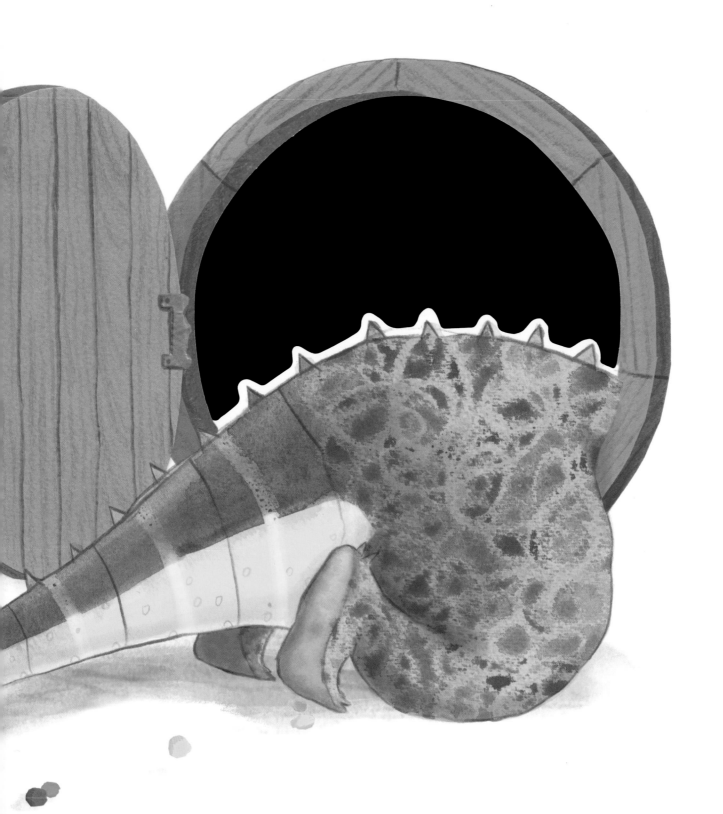

Let's see what's next door . . .

At last! Carter's home!
He looks very **happy**, doesn't he?

But it's not home for everyone.
Where should Carter's **friends** go?

Ah, I think they're off to have their own adventures.